A place of their very own

The sun shone through the hole in the roof like a spotlight. The house was a single big room, with stone walls, a stone floor, and a small fireplace on one wall. It was completely empty, if you didn't count the spider webs or the piles of dead leaves.

"I love it!" said Sara. "It's so romantic!"

"It's neat!" Beth said.

"There's something about it that feels kind of . . . special," Karen agreed. "Otherworldly."

Other books about the Fifth Grade Stars

Fifth Grade STARS

RENT-A-STAR

By Susan Saunders

Bullseye Books · Alfred A. Knopf
New York

To Annie Heithaus, for all her help

DR. M. JERRY WEISS, Distinguished Service Professor
of Communications at Jersey City State College, is the
educational consultant for Bullseye Books. Currently
chair of the International Reading Association
President's Advisory Committee on Intellectual
Freedom, he travels frequently to give workshops on
the use of trade books in schools.

A BULLSEYE BOOK PUBLISHED BY ALFRED A. KNOPF, INC.

Library of Congress Cataloging-in-Publication Data
Saunders, Susan. Rent a Star / by Susan Saunders.
p. cm.—(Fifth grade Stars ; #2) (A Bullseye book)
Summary: The Stars, a club of fifth-grade girls, hire
themselves out for odd jobs to earn money to fix up
their clubhouse, an old stone building on nearby
farmland, but discover that it is in danger of being
torn down by developers.
ISBN 0-394-89605-X [1. Clubs—Fiction.
2. Schools—Fiction.] I. Title. II. Series.
PZ7.S2577Re 1988 [Fic]—dc19 87-33116

RL: 5.6

Manufactured in the United States of America
1 2 3 4 5 6 7 8 9 0

◀ 1 ▶

The Clovers Get Amy Crazy

Amy Danner paid the cashier for her lunch, dropping the change into a see-through plastic pocketbook already crammed full with a purple styling brush, a pin that said BUMMER, a pink flamingo hair clip like the one stuck in her tight brown curls, and a key chain with I ♡ CHOCOLATE stamped on it. She picked up her tray and led the way across the noisy elementary school cafeteria to an empty table near the windows.

"I can't believe it—fish again!" she complained to Jan Bateman, who was right behind her. Amy set her tray down with a clatter. She rolled up both legs of her cartoon-printed jumpsuit to the tops of her

Converse All-Stars. "We've eaten so much fish," Amy went on, "I'm beginning to feel like a seal!" She flopped onto a folding chair and clapped her hands together to demonstrate.

"When you get the urge to balance a ball on your nose, then worry," Jan said with a grin, sliding onto the chair next to Amy's. Jan had straight brown hair with bangs, and she was wearing a green Crestview High sweatshirt. Her dad was head coach at Crestview, and her brother, Richie, was the star of the high school football team.

Jan took a bite of her fish patty. "It's not too bad. It could stand some herbs, though. Maybe some tarragon or thyme," she added, chewing slowly.

"When you're a famous chef with your own restaurant, maybe I'll eat smushed fish, but not before," Beth Greenfield said to Jan. "Until then, give me something I can recognize." Beth had brought her lunch from home that day—peanut butter and jelly on rye and a bag of barbecue potato chips— and so had her twin, Sara.

Beth and Sara had red hair and freckles. They were identical as long as they kept their mouths shut. As soon as they started to talk—or rather, *Beth* started to talk—it was easy to tell which was which. Sara was a watcher and a listener; she wanted to be a writer and was already working on a novel. Beth was gabby, and so nuts about animals that she was thinking of becoming a vet.

"It's the bun I object to more than anything." Karen Fisher, a tall blond girl with a thoughtful expression, was the last to sit down at their table. "It's kind of . . . sinister." She poked the bun on her plate suspiciously. "It reminds me of a story I read once, about a poisoner who worked in a bakery. . . . Or was it the one about UFOs from Cyndar Three that were disguised as fast food?"

"Speaking of invasions from outer space, here come Holly and the Clovers." Amy pointed to the front of the cafeteria line.

Practically everybody at River Grove Elementary—not least of all Holly herself—thought Holly Hudnut was the prettiest girl in school. She had a dimple in her cheek, a turned-up nose, and thick ash-blond hair that she wore in a glossy side ponytail. She even managed to make her shortness seem attractive—"I've always been petite," Amy could almost hear her saying.

Holly spent more money on clothes than half the fifth graders combined. She had some really nice stuff, like a leather bomber jacket. On the other hand, Amy thought, sometimes Holly looks like she just escaped from a fifties sitcom: *Father Knows Best* or maybe *Leave It to Beaver*. I wouldn't be caught dead in what she's got on today!

Holly was wearing a dark blue fuzzy sweater, a plaid pleated skirt, and brown penny loafers. She paused just inside the door, checking out who was where in the lunchroom. Her blue-eyed gaze slid toward the table where Amy and the others were sitting, and locked on. Holly said something to one of the girls standing next to her—the whole group had side ponytails. Then Holly stepped into the room.

"They're heading straight for us," said Jan. "Holly must have something to say that she wants us to overhear."

"Something she thinks will make us crazy," Beth said.

Sure enough, Holly sat down at the next table, with Brenda Wallace on one side of her, Mary Rose Gallagher on the other, and Sue Pinson facing them. "The Clovers deserve a clubhouse," Holly announced in her piercing voice. "Like the Masons, or the Mooses. That's what I told my parents last night."

"I wonder why she doesn't borrow the intercom from Mrs. Campesi for these news bulletins?" Amy muttered. Mrs. Campesi was the elementary school principal. Like many other adults, she thought Holly was just about perfect: pretty, a good student, super polite to grownups, a volunteer for everything.

"Don't give her the satisfaction of listening," Karen advised, examining her green salad.

But Amy couldn't help listening.

"What did your parents say?" Mary Rose was asking Holly, with a sideways glance at the neighboring table.

Holly gave a self-satisfied smile, showing her dimple. "They'll do anything I want, especially if I sniffle a little. They're going to give us the room over the garage!"

"Oh, Holly!" Sue Pinson squealed. "That's fabulous!" Sue was Brenda Wallace's cousin, and she was practically afraid to breathe without Brenda's permission. "Isn't it, Bren?"

"For sure!" Brenda rolled her eyes at the group at the next table, waiting for a reaction.

Brenda was Holly's second-in-command. Amy thought of her as the Terminator. Brenda said all the rude things Holly was thinking, leaving Holly smelling like a rose in front of her admirers at school.

"Ac-tu-ally," Brenda drawled, "a club without a clubhouse is a joke!"

"Oh, yeah?" Amy jumped to her feet, ready to give Brenda a piece of her mind. Jan grabbed the back of Amy's jumpsuit and pulled her back down.

"She means the Stars!" Amy struggled to stand up again.

"Brenda's just trying to get us going. It really bugs the Clovers that they aren't the only club in the fifth grade anymore," Jan murmured.

"That's right," the other girls agreed.

It was their first year at River Grove

Elementary. Jan, Karen, Beth and Sara, and Amy had all moved into houses in a new subdivision called Sugar Tree Acres. Since all five of them rode the same bus to school, they had been thrown together right from the beginning. And, pretty much from the beginning, Holly Hudnut decided they weren't Clovers material.

Since Holly was the prettiest girl in school, the most popular with the teachers, and rich, all the girls in the fifth grade at River Grove Elementary wanted to be in her club. Brenda was a charter member. Her family had as much money as Holly's —maybe more. Brenda even had her own Arabian mare, Missy.

Mary Rose had a horse too, although she wasn't as much of a horse freak as Brenda. Mary Rose was nice-looking and a good athlete. Her family had two houses, one in the middle of town, the other a weekend place. Sue Pinson was a mouse, but she was Brenda's cousin. She also got fantastic grades and did the other Clovers' homework when they were too busy to bother.

The new girls had started out with a strike against them, of course, because only farm kids lived out their way and rode to town on their bus. Sugar Tree Acres had been a farm itself before it was a subdivision. As far as Holly and the Clovers were concerned, all the kids on the route were hicks from the sticks.

Then there were the particulars. Amy could imagine just what Holly had thought about the five of them. First there was Jan Bateman. Jan had possibilities, because everyone in River Grove had heard of the Batemans. Mr. Batemen was Crestview High's head coach, and her brother, Richie, was always getting his name in the paper for throwing a long pass and saving the game. The thing was, Jan wanted to be a chef, not a famous athlete. In Holly's mind a chef was probably a cross between one of the ladies who served food to the school cafeteria lunch line and scruffy old Joe at the River Grove Diner.

Still, Holly had asked Jan to her birthday party right after school started—after all, Jan's brother was famous. But when Jan refused to dump on the Stars, Holly dropped her like a hot potato.

Next there was Karen Fisher. She was

blond, tall, and really very pretty, although she didn't seem to notice it. She was too busy being a brain, getting all *A*'s, even in math, and reading books every spare second: weird English mysteries and even weirder science fiction stories. "What can you expect?" Amy could almost hear Holly saying. "Both of her parents are scientists—you know, like Dr. Frankenstein or something!"

Then there were the twins: Beth talked too much, and Sara hardly talked at all. Beth was always picking up squashed toads and half-dead birds and trying to nurse them back to life in a clinic behind their house. Sara was in another world, constantly scribbling in a red notebook. She was writing a romance about shipwrecked lovers named Sean MacNeill and Tiffany Vandermere.

The Greenfields came from a big family that was getting bigger—there were four kids already, and Mrs. Greenfield was expecting another one. Sara and Beth were usually in charge of the laundry, so the twins' clothes looked a little spotty from time to time. Add to that curly red hair and freckles the size of dimes. . . . "Totally impossible!" Jan had actually overheard Brenda Wallace say as soon as she saw them. "Out of the question!"

Sara and Karen weren't exactly social— they were too wrapped up in their own interests to care very much about the Clovers. But Beth had cared. And Amy had cared most of all. At her old school in the city, she'd definitely been a part of the "in group." She'd belonged to the most popular club, the Go-Gos. But none of the stuff that had been cool at P.S. 7 seemed to appeal to the Clovers of River Grove. They frowned at her unmatched high-tops; they turned up their noses at her personally designed glitter T-shirts; they snickered at the jewelry she'd made out of nuts and bolts and spray-painted gold.

First Amy was surprised, then hurt, and finally furious. She was the one who had most wanted to form a new fifth-grade club, with Beth backing her up. Now that they had one, she was determined that the Stars—named for their bus route, the *Sugar Tree Acres Route*—would blow the Clovers away. And she wasn't going to take any garbage from Brenda Wallace!

"She'd better watch her mouth!" Amy scowled across the aisle at Brenda.

"Cool it, Amy," Beth said, dumping Karen's leftover green salad into her empty lunchbox to take home to her guinea pigs. "Which club would you rather belong to? The Clovers, with snobby old Holly and pushy Brenda and a clubhouse in the Hudnuts' garage? Or the Stars, without the clubhouse but with your four closest friends, who happen to be the neatest girls in school?"

"If you think the stupid Clovers mean beans to me, you're totally off the wall!" Amy said huffily.

Still, Amy thought about the Clovers' new clubhouse all through math and social studies, and then it was time for music. In fifth grade you could learn to play an instrument or you could sing in the chorus. Jan had chosen the saxophone, Karen the violin, and Beth the trumpet. But Amy had struggled through piano lessons in first and second grades, with hours of practice every week, and she wasn't going to repeat that mistake. She chose chorus, which should have been fine, because in chorus a whole group of kids just stood around and sang.

There was one major problem, however. Holly Hudnut thought she had the best voice in the fifth grade, in the whole elementary school, maybe in all of River Grove or possibly the world. And Holly was in the chorus.

◀ 2 ▶
Matthew Butts In

Sara had chosen chorus too, so Amy wasn't entirely alone. But Holly had Brenda and Mary Rose for company. The three of them clustered together on their way downstairs to the music room, their penny loafers keeping perfect time.

"We can have sleepovers out there"—the Clovers were still blabbing about their new clubhouse—"and real parties . . . play tapes as loud as we want, with no one around to bug us about it!" "Parties with dancing. And boys!"

Amy raised an eyebrow at Sara, who shook her head sadly. The Clovers were becoming completely boy-crazy. It was embarrassing.

"Coming through!" Pete McBride raced down the stairs, his spiky blond hair standing straight up. He bumped into Brenda on his way past. "Sorry, *Bren*!"

"Rrgh!" Brenda growled as he tore down the hall to the music room. "He is such a little rat!"

Amy and Sara giggled. Pete McBride happened to be short, but he was one of the cutest boys at River Grove Elementary. All of the Stars had gotten to know him because his family had been friendly with Jan's family for a long time. Pete loved to tease, especially the Clovers.

"*Squirrel,* you mean," Holly corrected Brenda with a smirk.

She had come up with names for Pete and his best friend, Matthew Ellis: Rocky and Bullwinkle, like the cartoon squirrel and moose. Amy hated giving Holly credit for anything, but she had to admit that the names kind of fit. Pete was small and was always racing around, acting a little . . . squirrelly, like Rocky. And Matthew was tall and skinny, with big ears, like Rocky's sidekick, Bullwinkle the moose.

"Why is Pete in such a hurry?" Amy wondered aloud to Sara. "He usually makes a point of being late to chorus."

The reason was clear as soon as they walked through the music room door. Pete was handing out sheets of paper with the words to a song written on them. "Amy . . . Sara . . ." He pretended he was going to hand a copy to Holly, then snatched it back. "Not you, Holly—this one has a *tune.* Everybody knows the tune, right? One, two, three. . . ."

As Pete and Amy and some of the other kids shouted the words to the Beastie Boys' "Fight for the Right to Party," Holly turned on her heel and stormed out of the room, with Brenda and Mary Rose in attendance. The singers had barely gotten to the second verse when the Clovers came back with Mr. Gill, the music teacher.

Mr. Gill was a thin, dry-looking man with a bald head and a small, bristly mustache. He clapped his hands together for quiet. "Pass those papers to the front, please, and turn to page thirty-four in your song-books. . . ."

Pete McBride groaned. " 'Climb Ev'ry Mountain' again? Give us a break, Mr. Gill. At least the Beastie Boys—"

"I'm sorry you don't approve of my musical selections, Peter," Mr. Gill interrupted. "But as they say in the business, tough darts. Hurry, hurry, class—we have so little time and quite a few songs to get through today," he added as the rest of the kids filed in. ". . . First we'll run through the sopranos' part, then the altos', and finally the baritones'."

Holly flipped back her ponytail and took her place at the front of the group, a smug smile on her face. Not only was she a soprano, she was the soprano *soloist* of the chorus.

"Soloists have to be able to sing two octaves or more: at least sixteen notes," she'd bragged to her friends, and to anyone else who cared to listen, at the beginning of the semester.

"She may sing sixteen notes," Pete McBride had whispered loudly. "But four or five of them sound exactly alike." Holly had had a fit, and Pete had ended up in the principal's office.

Mr. Gill rapped his knuckles on the top of the piano for attention. "All right, sopranos? Holly? Mary Rose? Sara?"

Amy was an alto if she was anything—her voice had more in common with the Beastie Boys.

Mr. Gill played a couple of chords on the piano. Then he launched into the melody, humming the sopranos' part as the girls sang along. "Climb . . . humm humm-humm-humm . . . ford . . . humm humm-humm."

Holly's voice rang out, loud and shrill, but about halfway through the song she seemed to lose first the melody and then the words. There was a strange droning sound coming from somewhere in the room: "You have to fight . . . for your right . . . to *pa-a-arty!*"

Holly fumbled for a few seconds before she stopped singing altogether. An unattractive scowl crept over her face.

Mr. Gill lifted his hands from the piano and sighed. "What is the problem, Holly?"

"It's Pete McBride, Mr. Gill!" Brenda was

pleased to do the snitching. "He's muttering so loud that Holly can't hear the music!"

"All right, Peter," Mr. Gill said wearily. "You know the way to Mrs. Campesi's office."

Brenda stuck out her tongue at Pete as he left the room.

The chorus stumbled through "Climb Ev'ry Mountain," "People," and "We Are the World," until finally school was over for the week.

. . .

"We'll go to Olsen's first," Holly said to Brenda as the last bell rang. "Buy some stuff for the clubhouse walls, and maybe two or three of those big tie-dyed floor pillows."

"Olsen's has a great poster of Rob Lowe," Mary Rose said. "Can I go with you? I know it'd be fine with my mom."

Holly nodded. "Sure. My mother will be picking us up at the side door."

. . .

Amy and Sara hurried up the stairs and out the front door to catch their bus. They had to squeeze past three of the younger kids who were racing up and down the aisle, ducking behind seats, trying to zap each other with water guns. Two sixth graders wearing baseball caps had portable radios blasting out rock and roll on different stations.

"Battle of the Bands!" one of them bellowed, turning his radio up even louder.

"The usual zoo!" Beth hollered over the noise. She and Jan and Karen were sitting on the back seat. Karen, her fingers stuffed in her ears, was reading a book.

Amy peered out the window. "There's Holly," she reported. "And Brenda and Mary Rose." The Clovers were walking over to Mrs. Hudnut's dark blue Mercedes. "They're on their way to Olsen's."

"Hi!" A boy plopped down so close to Amy that he almost sat on her leg. "Who are you glomming?"

"I'm not *glomming* anybody! Get off me, Matthew!" Amy snapped, giving him a shove that dumped him in the aisle.

Matthew Ellis lived in Sugar Tree Acres too, almost directly across the street from Amy's house. He sat in the seat in front of the girls and swiveled around to grin at her.

Matthew could have been a nerd. He was gangly, and his ears stuck out, and he seemed to be growing out of his clothes at the top and bottom before your very eyes. But he wasn't a nerd. Besides being best friends with Pete McBride, he was a golden-oldies expert: Matthew had a huge collection of old 45s that he'd found in junk stores and at yard sales, and he'd won just about every golden-oldies contest on WBRG/River Grove.

Matthew leaned forward, looking out the window in time to see Holly open the car door. "Cloners!" he hooted. That was the name he and Pete had given the Clovers, because they all tried to talk and dress and *be* exactly alike.

"Why, it's Bullwinkle Moose!" Holly said loudly. She splayed her fingers out on either side of her head, like antlers, and so did Brenda and Mary Rose. All three of them giggled.

Matthew sat down quickly, his face bright

red. "Uh . . . where's McBride?" he asked Amy to cover his embarrassment. "I haven't seen him since before chorus practice."

Amy was staring at the back of the Hudnuts' car as it pulled away—SUPRMOM, the license plate said—so Sara answered. "Pete messed up Holly's singing, and . . ."

"And she had him sent up the river." Matthew liked to talk like old gangster movies. "He's in the warden's office, right?"

A stream of water caught Matthew in the back of the head. "I'll get you for that, Kevin!" He lunged for a chubby kid with a crew cut and a yellow squirt gun.

"Boys are so childish," Amy said with a sigh.

The bus doors slammed shut, but Mrs. Purvis, the driver, didn't start the engine.

"Hey, why aren't we moving? It's the weekend! Let's go, let's go!" shouted the two sixth graders in baseball caps, stamping their feet at the same time.

"Keep it up, George and Lionel Hooley!" Mrs. Purvis yelled from her place behind the wheel. She pointed to a large sign that said RIDING THE BUS IS A PRIVILEGE. "We'll sit here until tomorrow morning unless everybody, and I mean everybody, pipes down and takes a seat!"

The bus went dead quiet as all the kids scrambled to sit down.

Matthew collapsed into the seat in front of Amy again. "So, what are you looking so waxy about?" he wanted to know.

"Are you in training to do detective work, or are you just plain nosy?" Amy said.

But Jan answered his question. "The Clovers are getting a real clubhouse," she explained.

"We're just as much of a club as they are, any day," Amy muttered. "But we live in Sugar Tree Acres, so we're out of luck— every house is either a ranch or a Colonial, everything's brand-new, and nobody has any spare rooms over old garages to turn into great clubhouses."

"There *are* some old buildings at Sugar Tree Acres," Matthew said.

"Sure. The farmhouse." Amy frowned at him. "Great idea, Matthew. Maybe we'll just buy one of the condos." Instead of knocking down the old house from Sugar Tree Acres' farming days, Piker and Wicket—they were the developers—were turning it into two large apartments.

"You lend us a hundred and twenty-five thousand dollars, and we'll have the best clubhouse in town," said Beth.

"Not the farmhouse," Matthew replied. "There's a funny little house back in the last strip of woods. It's kind of a mess, but it's got potential. You could fix it up." He smiled at Amy. "You're good at that."

Amy blushed, and then glared at him. Her mother and father were divorced, and Amy's mother had had to learn to do things for herself. She'd always told Amy that she wanted her daughter to be able to handle any emergency when she grew up, so Amy had taken classes in woodworking, rappeling down cliffs, first aid, making shelters in the wilderness, repairing small household appliances, maintaining a car, and lots of other things she'd just as soon not mention.

Amy wanted to be a fashion designer, not an electrician. Just because Matthew Ellis had once seen her rewiring a lamp. . . . "Don't you have anything better to do than spy on me?" she snapped.

"Oh . . . uh . . . I think it's neat that you can fix stuff," Matthew mumbled apologetically, and faced the front.

As the bus turned the corner, heading toward Sugar Tree Acres, Amy said to her friends, "Can you give me one good reason why the Clovers should have a fancy clubhouse and all we can come up with is a shack . . . besides the fact that they're rich and can have anything they want? It's not fair!"

◀ 3 ▶
A Clubhouse for the Seven Dwarfs

The Stars took turns having their Saturday afternoon meetings at one another's houses. At Jan's they stuffed themselves with her incredible double-fudge brownies and got to watch Richie lift weights. Amy thought fifth-grade boys were okay . . . for friends. But Richie looked a lot like King Zero, her favorite rock star.

Karen had the neatest room in the group, with white furniture, dark blue walls, tall bookcases full of things like rock crystals and fossilized fish and plants, and sky maps. She even had a lamp that beamed the constellations onto her ceiling when you turned the switch.

Amy's place was mostly beige: beige carpets, beige walls, beige furniture, even a beige dog. Amy *had* to wear wild clothes in self-defense. Since her mom was into natural foods and thought sugar was poison, Amy's house was not the place to eat anything. At Amy's the Stars spent a lot of time trying on makeup—her mother let her buy it and try it but not wear it anywhere.

The meetings at Sara and Beth's were usually the most interesting. Their two-story house was stuffed with kids and pets— two dogs, two guinea pigs, a turtle, a goldfish, and three cats—and you never knew what was going to pop out when you opened a closet or a drawer. Amy figured that one of the reasons Mr. Greenfield sold insurance was that he knew from experience just how full of surprises life could be.

That Saturday afternoon it was the Greenfields' turn to have the Stars over. The twins' little brother, Jeffrey, answered the door when Amy rang. "They're in the basement," he said. Then he roared off, making noises like a motorcycle, almost running over Clementine, the oldest cat in the world.

A woman had been carrying Clementine

in a cardboard box when she spoke to Beth on Main Street. "She's still a kitten," the woman had said, opening the top of the box just enough to let Beth see the striped cat inside. "Her name is Clementine. Unfortunately, I already have six cats and I can't afford to keep her. I'm on my way to the pound."

The pound? Beth knew she couldn't let that happen. There was always room for another pet at the Greenfields'. Beth had lugged the cat, still in the box, home on her bike.

The twins' little sister, Amanda, was the first to notice something peculiar about Clementine: she had no teeth. "Our kittens all had teeth when they were this size," Amanda pointed out.

The twins rushed the cat to their veterinarian, who informed them Clementine was probably the oldest living cat he'd ever seen. "So what were we supposed to do?" Beth said when she told the other girls about it. "Kick out the oldest cat in the world?"

Clementine was living on soft baby food and getting fat at the Greenfields'. She waddled across the living room and into the kitchen, with Amy slowly following her. Clementine sat down next to her food dish and meowed. She looked really disappointed when Amy walked down the stairs to the basement.

Jan and Karen were already there, curled up in old beanbag chairs. "Hi, Amy!" everyone said. Then they went back to what they'd been talking about: a clubhouse.

"I don't think there's anything wrong with taking turns at each other's houses," Karen said. "Do we have to do everything the Clovers do?"

"It would be nice to have a place of our own," Sara said wistfully. She shoved a spotted kitten away from the onion dip with her elbow while she finished braiding Amanda's hair. "A house in the woods sounds so . . . private."

"And Matthew Ellis likes it," Jan pointed out.

"Matthew Ellis thinks 'One-Eyed, One-Horned Flying Purple People Eater' is the best song ever written," Amy said. "If he likes it, forget it!"

"What's wrong with 'One-Eyed, One-

Horned Flying Purple People Eater'?" Karen said. "It's science fiction."

"Why don't we look at the house first, before we waste any more time arguing about it?" Jan suggested. "It may be such a wreck that we couldn't use it even if we wanted to."

"All in favor of checking it out right now?" said Beth.

"Aye," everyone answered.

"Great!" said Beth, jumping up and giving Amanda a push toward the stairs.

"But where is it, exactly?" Sara asked as she followed her sister.

"In the strip of woods that hasn't been cleared," Jan answered. "That's what Matthew said."

"Maybe we should call Matthew and get him to show us," Sara suggested.

Amy was tired of Matthew knowing everything she did. "Let's not! I'm sure we can find the house ourselves. We're not talking about a national forest; we're talking about Sugar Tree Acres." She grabbed a handful of peanut butter cookies before she started after the other girls.

At one time Sugar Tree Acres had been a good-sized farm, a large rectangle with the farmhouse and some barns in the center. Now there were new houses built on almost all of the land—except for a hilly back corner, covered with trees, with a muddy stream trickling through it.

The back corner was a short bike ride from the twins' house. When the Stars had braked their bikes at the bottom of the hill, Amy said, "Matthew Know-It-All Ellis didn't happen to mention that there's a tall fence around it. He is such a flake!"

"It's not a very solid fence," said Jan. "There are slats missing all over the place. It'd be easy enough to slip through."

"Who does this belong to? Aren't we going to be trespassing?" Sara asked a little nervously.

"Piker and Wicket—who else?" said Beth. "But so what? They're not using it for anything. It's too hilly to build on." She leaned her bike against the fence. "Let's go in."

The five girls squeezed through the fence and stood there for a moment, looking at the trees: maples, oaks, spruces, more maples. There were lots of bushes growing between them. Amy could see honeysuckle, mountain laurel, and, as soon as she stepped forward, brambles. . . . She rubbed a scratch on her hand. "Probably poison ivy, too," she murmured to herself as she detoured around a tangle of vines. "I don't see how there could be a house anywhere in this mess. If Matthew did this as a joke, I'll kill him!"

"Ick!" Jan had put her foot down on what looked like solid ground, only to discover that it was mushy. Thick brown mud closed over the toe of her sneaker. "It's like quicksand," she said. When she tugged her foot out, there was a loud sucking sound.

Karen gazed at the trees and bushes that surrounded them. "You know," she said in a faraway voice, "this reminds me of a story I read called 'Evil Lurks in Mystery Marsh.' The marsh was swampy and ringed with trees, just like this, and several people had disappeared without leaving a trace . . . except for their shoes."

It was spooky and kind of quiet inside the woods. The trees muffled sounds.

"I don't think I want to know any more

about that story, Karen," Sara said shakily. "Beth, maybe we should go get Skippy." Skippy was one of the Greenfields' dogs, half Airedale and half Labrador.

"Are you kidding?" her sister replied. "Skippy's afraid of his shadow!"

A twig snapped, and they all jumped.

"This is silly," said Amy, who had camped out once in the Utah wilderness, hundreds of miles from nowhere. "We're only about two minutes from home. Let's walk through these trees to the other side, and if we haven't found Matthew's phantom house, we'll forget the whole thing."

She set off through a thicket of small pines, walked around a slimy puddle, stepped into a clearing, and there it was! The little house was gray and square, with a high, peaked roof. The walls were still standing, and probably would be for a long time to come, because they were solid stone. There was a wooden front door—shorter than the normal size—five small windows, and a crooked chimney.

Sara gasped. "It's beautiful! Tiffany Vandermere would love this house!" Tiffany was the beautiful red-headed heroine of

Sara's novel. Sara pulled her red notebook out of her pocket and scribbled a few lines.

"I think it belongs to the Seven Dwarfs," Amy said. "And they must have been away from home for a long time, because this place is a disaster! The windows are broken, the roof has a big hole in it, the inside has got to be a mess from leaks and stuff. . . ." Amy knew enough about fixing things to realize just *how much* of a wreck it was.

Karen looked in through one of the windows and shook her head. "It's not so bad," she reported. "The floor's made of some kind of rock—slate, maybe. I don't think rain can ruin slate."

Beth tried the door. "It's not locked. The knob turns." She shoved hard against the door with her shoulder. "It's just stuck . . . because the wood . . . is swollen!" The door burst open with a crash, and the girls crowded inside.

The sun shone through the hole in the roof like a spotlight. The house was a single big room, with stone walls, a stone floor, and a small fireplace on one wall. It was completely empty, if you didn't count the spider webs or the piles of dead leaves.

"I love it!" said Sara. "It's so romantic!"

"It's neat!" Beth said.

"There's something about it that feels kind of . . . special," Karen agreed. "Otherworldly."

"Listen, I know I started the whole thing about having a clubhouse," Amy began, "but this isn't going to work. We had to practically hack through a jungle to get here. . . ."

"Maybe Mom would let us bring the beanbag chairs over," Sara told her sister. "And some curtains."

"There's no electricity!" Amy went on, hoping the other girls would snap out of it.

"Everything we'd need runs on batteries—lights, radios," Beth said. "And we'd mostly be here in the daytime, anyway."

"What about heat? With these stone walls and floors, we'd freeze to death," Amy argued. The Clovers probably had central heating!

"There's a fireplace," said Karen.

"But there are five broken windows, and a giant hole in the roof!" said Amy.

"We'll fix it," said Beth.

"You know how to do that stuff, Amy," Sara said. "You can show us."

"Maybe I can make a bookcase, but I sure don't know how to fix a hole in a roof!" Amy exclaimed.

Karen looked around the room. "A bookcase would be nice in that corner," she said dreamily.

Sometimes Karen could be a real space cadet!

◀ 4 ▶
Rent-a-Star

"What we've got here is a dump!" Amy was counting on Jan to say something sensible and back her up.

But what did Jan say? "There's always Uncle Robert. . . ."

Amy was almost afraid to ask. "Who's Uncle Robert?"

"My mom's youngest brother. He's the foreman for a construction company. We always call him up when we need him to fix things around the house."

"All ri-i-ight!" Beth exclaimed.

"Even with Uncle Robert, how would we pay for all the stuff he'd have to buy for repairs?" Amy asked.

"It's only five windows, and a patch for the roof," Karen said blithely. "We'll get jobs after school and on weekends."

"Most people think fifth graders are too young to be baby-sitters," Sara told her.

"It doesn't have to be baby-sitting. I'm not used to little kids, anyway." Karen was an only child, like Amy. "We can do odd jobs, like cleaning junk out of attics or neatening up basements."

"Walking dogs or cat-sitting," Beth suggested.

"I could weed gardens," Sara said.

"And I could make birthday cakes," said Jan. "I'm getting pretty good at frosting."

Amy sighed, beaten. "I guess I could re-wire lamps or fix toasters."

"We'll have to advertise," Jan told them. "We'll put notices up at the grocery store and on the library bulletin board."

"What'll we say about ourselves? 'Odd Jobs by the Stars'?" asked Beth.

"What about 'Rent-a-Star'?" Amy found herself getting into the spirit, in spite of herself.

"Perfect!" The other girls clapped.

"We'll list some of the things we can do. . . ."

"Charge two dollars an hour for each of us. . . ."

"Or according to the job. . . ."

"And we'll give all our telephone numbers, with 'please call after six' written underneath."

"With all five of us working, we'll make enough money to fix the place up in a few weeks!" Beth said as they took a last look around. "The Clovers can have their old garage. We'll have a real house!" She pulled the door closed behind them. "I wonder why this door is so small?"

Karen shrugged. "It's an old house. People were shorter in those days."

. . .

Jan told them she'd call her uncle Robert when she got home.

"What did he say?" Amy asked her as they spoke on the telephone later that evening.

" 'No problem!' " Jan replied. "That's what he always says. He'll meet us at the clubhouse after school next Wednesday."

．．．

On Sunday the Stars rode downtown on their bikes to stick up the notices Karen had printed: one at Handy Grocery, others at Miller's Deli, the Beverage Barn, and the River Grove Public Library.

To get to the library bulletin board they walked through the sliding glass doors, past the check-out desk, and toward the children's wing. "We're looking a little disheveled here," said Mrs. Dawson, the head librarian. "This knitting seminar is three months out of date, and I know Mr. Johnson's briefcase has long since been found. . . ." She removed two notices and took the one Karen was holding.

" 'Rent-a-Star,' " she read aloud. "What a cute idea!"

"We're trying to make some money to fix up our clubhouse," Beth told her.

Mrs. Dawson nodded. "We'll put you right next to the poster for the book sale and fair."

"You're having a book sale?" Karen edged closer to the poster. She'd found some of her favorite mysteries at used-book sales.

"That's right," Mrs. Dawson replied.

"Weekend after next, to raise funds for the expansion of the children's wing."

"What's this, Mrs. Dawson?" Amy pointed to a list of names.

The librarian started to explain. "Those are the people who will have booths at the—"

But she was interrupted by a shrill voice. "Hi, Mrs. Dawson—we've come to sign up for the book fair."

"Why, hello, Holly!" Mrs. Dawson stepped aside so Holly could add a name to the list, and Holly printed THE CLOVERS in capital letters with a pink felt-tip pen. "Thank you," said Mrs. Dawson. "I don't know how the library would manage without the Hudnuts. Your mother has done a wonderful job as chairman of the building committee. . . ."

"Amy Danner!" Brenda Wallace exclaimed practically in Amy's ear. "I didn't expect to find *you* in the library."

"Meaning what?" Amy said coldly.

"Well, I know the . . . um . . . the *Stars*"—she smirked as she said the name—"have a couple of bookworms for members." Brenda pointed at Karen and Sara, who were browsing avidly through the shelves already. "But you, too?"

"For your information, we're here to sign up for the book fair!" Amy could have bitten her tongue as soon as she'd said it.

"Amy!" Beth muttered.

"Oh, you are? What are you selling in your booth?"

"Uh . . ." What could they sell? "Food," Amy said quickly.

"Food! Bo-o-oring. We're selling horseback rides," Brenda said snootily. "I'm donating Missy for the day."

Brenda was always talking about her horse—she even carried Missy's picture in her wallet.

"Children can't resist horseback rides." Holly had joined them. "We'll probably make enough money to buy a lamp, or a desk, or something really major. They'll put our name on it—'The Clovers'—on a little gold plate."

Amy took a deep breath and plunged in again. "Gee, all we've got is Jan's secret recipe for double-fudge brownies," she said sarcastically. She heard Jan groan behind her, but she couldn't seem to stop herself.

"We're interested in buying a filmstrip projector for the library."

Holly smiled sweetly, realizing Amy had gotten the Stars into a bind. "Well, then—why don't you sign up? Use my pen!"

Holly handed Amy her felt-tip, and she and Brenda watched closely as Amy scribbled THE STARS right under THE CLOVERS on the list.

"Thank you, girls. I'll have to get the particulars from you on the size and shape of your booth," said Mrs. Dawson. "But aren't you going to be awfully busy, with the book fair on top of the jobs you'll be taking to fix up your clubhouse?"

"Your clubhouse!" The looks on Holly's and Brenda's faces almost made everything worthwhile for Amy.

"That's right, Holly," said Jan. "We have our own clubhouse at Sugar Tree Acres."

"It's nothing large, but it's a separate building, with its own fireplace," Beth added casually.

"It has a fireplace?" Brenda said in a choked voice.

"It needs work, but it's very solid—stone

walls. Houses were built to last in the old days," said Karen.

"An old stone house?" Holly said disbelievingly.

"Holly! Brenda! We have to go, girls!" It was Mrs. Hudnut, a large, noisy woman in a tweed suit, calling from the door.

Holly tore her eyes away from Karen's face. "Be right there, Mom," she said. She glanced at the Stars' notice on the bulletin board on her way out and managed one last zinger: "Do you do bathrooms, girls?"

"I'd jump off the Empire State Building before I'd do anything for *you*, Holly Hudnut!" Amy retorted, scowling at her retreating back.

"Your booth?" Mrs. Dawson said when she came back from her office with a thick brown notebook. "Do you have any idea how much space you'll need for it?"

"We have to think about it," Jan said, to get Amy off the hook. "We'll let you know next week, Mrs. Dawson."

As they filed out of the library, Amy apologized. "I see Holly and Brenda, and my mouth seems to take on a life of its own. I'm really sorry, guys."

"That's okay. We'll just have to make lots of brownies," Jan said.

"I'm glad we're doing something for the library," Sara added.

"I loved seeing Brenda change colors," said Beth.

"She reminds me of Mrs. Merkle in *Ten Birds with One Stone*," Karen said slowly. "Mrs. Merkle was a multiple murderer. She had brown hair and a horse, just like Brenda, and she . . ."

◀ 5 ▶
A Real Challenge

The Stars had their first job that Monday. A woman had called Amy's number on Sunday night. "Hello. Is this Rent-a-Star?" she asked.

"Yes, it is," Amy said, grabbing paper and a pencil. "May I help you?"

"I certainly hope so," the woman said. "My name is Mrs. Ross, and I'm having problems with mice."

"Oh, we're not exterminators," Amy said quickly.

"I understand that," Mrs. Ross said. "But until someone cleans up my attic and takes away the trash, I'll never be able to get rid of the mice. What I'd like you to do is put everything into garbage bags and carry them down to the curb. I'm not strong enough myself. Do you think you could manage?"

"Definitely," said Amy. "We charge—"

"Two dollars an hour each—I saw your ad at Miller's," Mrs. Ross said.

"And we work only after school, or on weekends."

"That's fine with me. I must warn you that this may take you several days, even with two or three people working. I can't remember the last time I cleared out my attic."

"No problem," said Amy. The longer they worked, the more money they'd make. "Is tomorrow afternoon at three thirty all right?"

"I'll be expecting you," said Mrs. Ross, sounding relieved. "My address is 35 Post Street. It's a shingled house with a large maple in front." Post Street was in one of the older neighborhoods in River Grove.

Jan's dad had scheduled a tennis lesson for her on Monday afternoon—he was still hoping to turn her into a prize-winner like Richie—so she wouldn't be able to help.

· 48 ·

Karen's grandmother was visiting, which meant she was out too. Amy dialed the Greenfields.

"We've got our first job!" she told Beth. Amy explained about Mrs. Ross's attic. "Can you and Sara go there with me after school?"

"I think so. Hang on. Let me check with Mom." Beth put down the phone with a clatter. Amy could hear Clementine meowing in the background and a children's song about whales on the stereo, with Amanda singing along loudly. Jeffrey, still pretending to be a motorcycle, varoomed past the telephone.

Then Beth was back. "It's okay with her. She has to take Amanda to the dentist anyway, so she can give us a ride to Mrs. Ross's house."

"Great!" said Amy. "My mom'll pick us up on her way home from work." Amy's mother was a lawyer, and she worked at Kemper, Keeler, and Sloan, just off Main Street. "Better bring old shirts or something to wear over your school clothes. It's probably pretty dusty up there."

The twins brought more than that. When they got on the bus the next morning, Beth was carrying a wire cage about the size of a shoebox.

"What's that for?" Amy asked. She and Jan and Karen were sitting together near the front of the bus. Matthew Ellis was in back, minding his own business for once.

"It's an Allgood trap," Beth answered. "I started thinking about those poor mice at Mrs. Ross's, and exterminators, and everything, and I thought we could try this."

"Beth used it at our old house," Sara added. "It catches them alive."

•   •   •

When the Stars walked into the classroom, Brenda was standing near Sue's desk, going over math problems. Holly was leaning against the bookshelves at the back of the room, sending meaningful glances to Clifford Hargrove III. Cliff was good-looking, with reddish-blond hair and green eyes, and his father was the president of the River Grove National Bank. Holly thought Cliff was the only boy in the fifth grade good enough for her. He was the most conceited person Amy had ever met.

Mary Rose was facing the door, and she

spotted the wire trap right away. "What's that thing?" she asked Beth.

Before Amy could say "a bird cage," or something else harmless, Mr. Carson put down his paper and spoke up. Mr. Carson was their teacher. He was a nice man but not always a help.

"That's an animal trap," he said, giving Beth an approving smile. "You put slices of cheese or fruit inside. The animal goes in after them, squeezing through this funnel. He's not hurt, but he can't get back out."

"And you have a cage full of live rats? Gross!" said Mary Rose.

"This is for *mice!*" Beth exclaimed indignantly.

"You take the mice to a park or an empty lot and release them," Mr. Carson continued. "There's the bell. Let's settle down, class."

"Are you catching rats as an odd job?" Brenda hissed at Beth during silent reading.

"Or are you trying to get some new members for your club?" murmured Holly.

She and Brenda and Mary Rose snickered. Beth's face turned an angry red, and

Amy felt her own ears burning. The Stars would show the Clovers, all right—they'd have the fanciest clubhouse in town, if Amy personally had to work her fingers to the bone to fix it!

After school that day she and the twins piled into the back of the Greenfields' messy station wagon, along with Amanda and Jeffrey and Herkie the turtle. Mrs. Greenfield dropped them off at 35 Post Street.

"Wow!"said Beth as the car pulled away. "It's huge!"

The big, white, shingled house was three stories tall, with a tower on one end and a wraparound porch. The front door opened as the girls started up the walk, and a small, gray-haired woman looked at them sharply.

"You're on time," she said, sizing them up. "And you've brought a mousetrap." She had pink-and-white skin crisscrossed with tiny wrinkles, keen brown eyes, and a no-nonsense expression. "I'm Mrs. Ross, and you are . . ."

"Amy, Beth, and Sara." Amy introduced herself and the twins.

"You're younger—and smaller—than I expected," said Mrs. Ross. "And I can't abide noise."

"Oh, we're strong," Beth assured her.

"And very quiet," Sara added timidly.

"All right, Amy, Beth, and Sara—I'll put you straight to work. And we'll see. . . ."

Mrs. Ross led them into the house, across an entry hall hung with paintings of women in long dresses and men in three-piece suits, and up the stairs.

She took the stairs one at a time, stopping for just a second on each step. "I'm sorry I can't take you to the attic," she said when they'd gotten to the second floor. "The stairs are too steep for me."

"Oh! What a terrific cat!" Beth exclaimed.

An enormous cream-colored Persian with golden eyes strolled out of a bedroom, yawning and stretching.

"This is Lily," Mrs. Ross said. "Unfortunately, she's too fat and lazy to catch any mice, but she's good company. Maybe she'll guide you."

Mrs. Ross took a box off a small table and handed it to Amy. "Here are some garbage bags," she said, "and there are more in the kitchen. Just start filling them up. You'll find old newspapers and magazines, clothes and shoes, some furniture, dishes. . . . I can't begin to remember what's up there!"

"Is there anything you especially want to keep?" Beth asked her.

"At my age, I'm more interested in clearing out than in keeping," Mrs. Ross replied. "If you see something you're not sure about, you may ask me."

Lily was climbing the stairs to the attic, twitching her big fluffy tail back and forth, so Amy and Beth and Sara followed her. "There's a light switch at the top on the left," Mrs. Ross called after them.

Amy found the switch, flicked it on . . . and caught her breath. "Kowabunga!" she said at last.

"Wow!" murmured Beth. "I've never seen so much stuff!"

There were magazines piled waist-high, mounds of yellowed newspapers, and stacks of dusty books. There was a wall of cardboard boxes tied together with string, and two wooden wardrobes bursting with clothes. There was a row of tin trunks and cedar chests at one end of the attic, and a crowd of broken chairs, leaning coatracks, empty picture frames, and cracked mirrors at the other.

Lily lay down on a box and closed her eyes.

"Now what?" said Sara.

"I'll set up the trap." Beth picked her way between boxes and chairs to put the trap down in a corner. She baited it with a slice of apple from the school lunch ("tuna fish on a roll, vegetable sticks, whole milk, and chilled fruit").

Then Amy slipped on an oversize "Save the Whales" T-shirt that her mother sometimes slept in, and the twins buttoned up two of Mr. Greenfield's old office shirts. They unfolded garbage bags and shook them out.

"Ready?" asked Amy.

"Ready," the twins answered.

"Newspapers first."

They worked hard and as fast as they could. Still, they'd hardly finished bagging all the newspapers and magazines when Amy's mother honked her car horn out in front of the house.

They dragged the last bags to the head of the stairs and turned off the light. Mrs. Ross was waiting for them on the second floor. "How are you doing up there?" she asked.

"It's going to take a while," Amy told her.

Mrs. Ross nodded. "I expect to see you all tomorrow at the same time, girls. Keep track of your hours."

As they let themselves out, Beth said, "Two hours times three of us, six hours times two dollars an hour—that's twelve dollars already!"

"Hi, Mom!" Amy jumped into the front seat and the twins into the back of Celia Danner's minivan.

"Hello, sweetie. Hi, Beth, Sara." Ms. Danner leaned forward to look up through her windshield at the big house. "I didn't realize that your Mrs. Ross was *this* Mrs. Ross."

"What do you mean, '*this* Mrs. Ross'?"

"Mrs. Evelyn Ross, who was a Topping before she married," her mother explained. "The Toppings were one of the founding families of River Grove—they've been here longer than the town has."

"And so has the trash in their attic," murmured Beth from the back seat.

◀ 6 ▶
Another Suggestion from Matthew

Amy was still tired the next morning, and her back and arms ached from the lifting and bagging she and the twins had done the afternoon before. She wasn't in any mood to have a long conversation with Matthew Ellis at the bus stop, so she waited inside her house until she saw Mrs. Purvis pull up at the corner. Then she raced down the sidewalk and up the steps of the bus and sat down between Jan and Karen.

Matthew wasn't easily discouraged, however. He plopped down across the aisle, in front of Beth and Sara. When Jan asked them about the job, he was all ears.

"The attic is full of junk—everything you

can imagine," Amy told Jan. "We're stuffing it into bags for the garbage collectors to take away."

"You're actually throwing it out?" said Matthew in disbelief.

"It's trash!" Amy said. "Old magazines, books without covers, shoes thirty or forty years out of date—"

Matthew interrupted her with a groan. "You're doing this work to make money to fix up the house I told you about, right?" When Amy glared at him without answering, he added, "That's what Jan said yesterday. Anyway, if you're trying to make money, why are you throwing out the stuff? You've got a gold mine there!"

"What gold mine?" Karen asked him.

"You can get as much as five or six dollars for an old *Life* magazine," Matthew told the girls. "I should know. I'm always poking around junk stores and checking out yard sales, looking for 45s." He peered sharply at Amy. "You didn't find any records up there, did you? You're not throwing out records?"

Amy shook her head.

"Clothes—another popular item," Matthew went on. "See this shirt?" He was wearing a hideous long-sleeved tan shirt with big olive-green squares on it.

"I paid three dollars for this shirt, and it was *damaged*—hole in the elbow." He raised his arm to show them the sleeve. "My mom sewed it up. Are there any clothes in that attic?"

"Sure—tons of them," Amy said. "Along with broken chairs and cracked mirrors . . ."

"Antiques," said Matthew solemnly. "Valuable antiques."

"I think Matthew's right," Sara said.

"But will Mrs. Ross go for it?" Beth wondered aloud.

"All she's interested in is getting rid of everything in her attic, right? So it shouldn't matter to her how we get rid of it," said Amy. "We'll ask her this afternoon."

Looking very pleased with himself, Matthew Ellis leaned back in his seat and fiddled with the controls on his Walkman.

. . .

"A yard sale to raise money for your clubhouse," said Mrs. Ross. "Where did you intend to hold it?"

"We haven't really thought about that," Amy admitted. "We wanted to talk to you first."

"We'd have it at one of our houses," Beth said. "Besides Sara and Amy and me, there are two more girls in the Stars— Jan and Karen. We live in Sugar Tree Acres."

"My mom has a van, Beth and Sara's family has a station wagon, and Mr. Bateman, Jan's father, has a truck. We could haul everything away, making a few trips." Amy planned out loud.

"When would you have this sale?" Mrs. Ross asked.

"A week from Saturday? That would give us some time to get ready for it," Beth suggested. "We'd pick the stuff up that Friday evening."

"Well . . . I guess that would be all right," said Mrs. Ross. "I've waited this long. A week or so more shouldn't make any difference."

"Thank you so much, Mrs. Ross. We really

appreciate this," Amy said. "We'll put more notices up."

"And maybe two or three lines in the *River Grove Courier,* under 'Articles for Sale'?" said Beth.

"Let's not waste any more of Mrs. Ross's time," Amy said hastily. She didn't want the old lady to change her mind!

"Right. We'll get upstairs and get started," said Beth.

Lily was lounging on top of the Allgood, washing her face. She barely blinked as the girls dashed into the attic.

"No mice," said Amy. "Do you think this trap really works?"

"What mousetrap would work with a fat cat sitting on top of it?" Beth said. She moved Lily onto a box, took out the shriveled apple slice, and put in some school-lunch carrot sticks ("macaroni and cheese, carrot sticks, and bread and butter").

The girls pulled open the garbage bags they'd filled the day before.

"There must be a hundred old magazines in this one," Sara said. "At five dollars each, that's—"

"Let's not count on getting rich," Amy warned.

"I think we should have the yard sale at our place," announced Beth, dumping the magazines onto the floor again.

Her sister agreed. "We've got the biggest yard." Their house was on a large corner lot.

"And we're so messy anyway that a little more stuff won't matter," said Beth. "Can you imagine even a blade of grass out of place at Karen's?" The Fishers were the neatest family Beth had ever met.

"Would it be okay with your parents?" Amy asked the twins. Her own mom was great, but Amy wasn't sure she'd welcome a yard full of old junk.

"Sure. Mom loves yard sales," Beth answered. "Maybe we'll get rid of some of our trash too."

"More likely add to it," said Sara. "This is going to be fun!" She dug into a mound of dusty books. "Tomorrow we'll bring stickers and start putting prices on everything."

"Uh-uh. Tomorrow Jan's uncle Robert is

coming to the clubhouse," Amy reminded her. "We'll have to skip a day here."

Karen had accepted a job for the next afternoon, dog-sitting a toy poodle while his owner was having her hair done. "My regular sitter is on vacation, and Frisco can't bear to be alone," the woman had told Karen on the phone. "He gets so frantic that he completely destroys the place."

"I couldn't turn her down," Karen explained. "She sounded absolutely desperate—a little like Helena Syms in *The Dog Only Barked Twice,* and *she* needed all the help she could get, poor woman. . . ."

Karen was walking to her dog-sitting job after school, but Amy and Sara and Beth rode their bikes to Jan's house. They hadn't been there five minutes when Uncle Robert rang the doorbell.

"Four good-lookin' ladies!" he exclaimed when he saw them. "How lucky can a guy get?"

Amy had expected an *uncle* . . . but Uncle Robert was a *hunk*! He was about six feet tall, with broad shoulders, dark curly hair, and a mustache: not a stiff little brush like their music teacher Mr. Gill's, but a soft, curly mustache that turned up when he smiled.

He offered both of his arms. "May I escort you to my limousine?"

Uncle Robert's pickup truck had a front seat so wide that all five of them could fit without much crowding.

"He's incredible looking!" Amy whispered to Jan.

"Like Sean MacNeill," Sara murmured. Maybe I should give Sean a mustache, she added to herself.

"He has about a zillion girlfriends," Jan whispered back. "First left, Uncle Robert," she said out loud. "Then around the Crescent, and a right."

They pulled up next to the wooden fence and got out. Uncle Robert took a metal box from behind the seat—"my traveling toolbox," he called it—and squeezed through the fence after the girls.

Amy recognized the tangle of vines, the grove of small pines, the slimy puddle. This time she led the group straight to the clearing where the little gray house stood.

"Ah-hem." Uncle Robert examined each

of the broken windows, thumping the frames with his fingers. He stepped onto a stump and peered at the roof from the outside, humming to himself.

"Why do I feel as though I'm at Dr. Jackson's office for a checkup?" Beth whispered as they waited for a verdict.

Uncle Robert pushed open the front door and studied the hole in the roof from the inside. He took a steel tape measure out of his pocket, held it up near the hole, and then jotted some figures on a slip of paper.

Next he crouched down and stuck his head into the chimney. The girls heard him sneeze, and he pulled his head out. Then he just strolled around, running his hands over the blocks of cut stone that formed the walls of the house. Finally he stopped in the middle of the room and smiled at the girls.

"What do you think, Uncle Robert?" Jan asked. "Can we fix it?"

"They just don't make houses like they used to," Uncle Robert said. "We can fix it— no problem. The windows . . . piece of cake. The frames are solid oak, no dry rot. All we have to do is replace the glass panes, squirt a little caulking around them. The hole in the roof—that's gonna take a little more work. We'll have to buy a thick sheet of plywood to plug it up and then some roofing material to cover the plywood. The pattern is old, but I'll try to match the color. . . ."

"Uncle Robert, how much is this going to cost?" Jan asked anxiously.

"Let me see—glass . . ." Uncle Robert scribbled more numbers on the slip of paper. "Outdoor plywood . . . hmmm." He looked up at the girls and tugged at his mustache. "It'll probably come to around a hundred and fifty, a hundred and seventy-five dollars. But I don't want you to worry about it," he said in the next breath. "I'm offering you a long long-term loan. You can pay me back when you get out of college."

"You won't have to wait *that* long," Amy said.

"I think we'll be able to handle it," said Beth.

"We're having a giant yard sale a week from this Saturday," Sara told him.

"Not a week from Saturday!" Jan exclaimed. "We can't! That's the library book fair. I thought you meant the Saturday *after*!"

"Oh no!" Amy groaned. "We were so caught up in the yard sale that we completely forgot the library!"

"We have hundreds of brownies to bake," Jan reminded her. "And we have to come up with some kind of booth to sell them in."

"We can't really ask Mrs. Ross if we can postpone the yard sale until the following weekend. This all started because she wanted her attic cleaned out as soon as possible," Beth said.

"Then what about canceling the booth at the book fair?" Jan suggested.

"No!" the other three practically shouted.

"We'd look like jerks in front of Holly and the Clovers!" said Beth.

"Mrs. Dawson is counting on us," Sara pointed out.

"We'll get everything organized at Mrs. Ross's by next Wednesday. We can bake the brownies on Thursday afternoon and keep them in the refrigerator till Saturday, can't we?" said Amy.

"Three of us can work at the yard sale, and two at the library," Sara said.

"Or we'll take turns. We can do it," Beth declared.

But could they?

◀ 7 ▶

The Clovers Drop In

Uncle Robert bought the plywood for the roof and told Jan that he would start working on it that weekend. "I don't want you girls to see the clubhouse again until I've made some repairs," he said. "I'll give you a ring when I'm ready. And no peeking."

The Stars didn't have time to peek, anyway. Besides school and homework and the usual chores, they got calls to weed a garden, scrape and paint a shed, and wash three cars. They also got a personal and urgent request from Richie Bateman to clean up his room at the going rate of two dollars an hour.

"Uh-uh. Not me!" Jan said when her

brother asked if she would do it. "Not even for *six* dollars an hour!"

But Karen checked out the closet crammed with balled-up sweatsuits, the pile of running shoes under the bed, and the jumble of barbells and weights in the corner. "It'll be a challenge," she said. It took her two hours. She made four dollars and fifty cents for the Stars' building fund: the extra fifty cents was because Richie was so pleased with the work. Now the Stars had thirty-eight dollars and fifty cents to give to Uncle Robert.

Whoever wasn't out on a call that week helped Amy—she was still putting prices on things at Mrs. Ross's.

"A moose head?" Jan asked, holding it up.

It was Sunday afternoon, and just she and Amy were in the attic. The twins were babysitting Amanda and Jeffrey—"For free!" Beth grumbled—and Karen and her parents were at some kind of science conference in the city.

The moose head had shiny glass eyes that had faded from brown to blue, and a pleasant expression. "He's kind of cute, but a little moth-eaten," Amy said. "Let's see . . . seven fifty?"

She pulled more clothes out of the trunk she was unpacking. "What about this dress?" she asked.

The dress was shiny green silk, with a big silk rose at the hip. "It's hard to believe people actually wore this stuff," Amy murmured, holding the dress over her Road Warrior sweatshirt. "How do I look?"

"I think it's kind of elegant," said Jan. "Five dollars?"

"And this shirt?" It was yellow, with tiny red and blue ducks flying across it.

Jan giggled. "Matthew Ellis would probably give ten dollars for it. Anyone else wouldn't pay more than a dollar fifty."

Amy wrote $1.50 on a white sticker and stuck it to the collar of the shirt. "But if Matthew buys it, we'll have to look at it on him at least once a week. Remind me to hide it when he comes to the sale." She added the shirt to the pile of marked clothing. "That's it for this trunk."

Amy pushed the trunk aside so she could reach the chest behind it, and a picture frame crashed to the floor. "I can't believe it didn't break," she murmured, lifting it up. She wiped the dust off the glass with a piece of newspaper and looked at the drawing. "Hey, Jan—it's a map of River Grove in 1879!"

The girls carried the map over to the window to study it more closely. The roads were drawn to look like real roads, not the thin black lines that usually stood for roads on maps. There were groups of trees drawn here and there, and horses and buggies. Houses and stores lined the roads on either side.

"The names are written underneath," Jan said. "Here's Main Street. I recognize this building on the corner of Main and Fifth. 'Thomas Mackey and Sons, Haberdashers,' it says. Now it's the First National Bank of River Grove."

"Yeah, and here's the building Sparks Pharmacy is in. It was a hardware store in 1879," said Amy.

"The library's in the same place, even though it looks totally different. The old one had columns in front, and a big round window. Here's Post Street. . . . Wow! Here's *this* house!" said Jan.

Halfway down Post Street the artist had drawn a dark red house with a tower. HERBERT L. TOPPING was printed below it. "My mom said Mrs. Ross was a Topping, remember?" Amy said. "Maybe some of this junk is a hundred years old!"

"Is Sugar Tree Acres Farm on the map?" Jan traced Roanoke Avenue away from the center of town, taking the same route their school bus did.

"No." Amy shook her head. "The only thing there in 1879 was the J. D. Ellison estate." She pointed to a drawing of a large house with a circle of pine trees around it.

"This map would look great in the clubhouse, wouldn't it?" said Jan.

"Definitely, right over the fireplace. I think we'd better ask Mrs. Ross if she wants to keep it, though. It's got her house on it," Amy replied.

· · ·

"I haven't seen this in ages," Mrs. Ross said when they took the map downstairs to show her. "It isn't an original drawing—it's just a print—but it's attractive."

"It doesn't have Sugar Tree Acres on it, but I think our clubhouse is right around here somewhere." Amy put her finger down at the edge of the map, near the Ellison estate. "It's old too."

"Is it really?" Mrs. Ross sounded interested. "Tell me about it."

"Oh, it's built of gray stone, with a kind of small front door," Amy began.

"And a crooked chimney, and a fireplace inside," Jan went on.

"It's got a hole in the roof, and some broken windows, but Jan's uncle Robert is working on it, and we're raising money to pay for the materials," Amy finished.

Mrs. Ross nodded, gazing thoughtfully at the map. "Then you may have this for your clubhouse. And I've been meaning to talk to you about something else. . . . Wouldn't it be much more sensible if you had the yard sale here?"

"But Mrs. Ross!" Amy couldn't have been more surprised if Mrs. Ross had invited her to a rock concert. "There would be lots of cars parked out front, and people on your lawn, and *noise*. . . ."

"It would be your job to keep the crowd down near the curb so I wouldn't be bothered," Mrs. Ross said.

"Oh, we will!" said Amy. Post Street was not far from Main Street, where everyone went shopping on Saturdays in River Grove. They would attract so many more customers! And Mrs. Ross's house was close to the library, too, so the girls could easily go back and forth from the yard sale to the book fair. "You won't hear a sound!" Amy vowed.

"And thank you for being so nice!" said Jan enthusiastically.

Mrs. Ross nodded briskly. "It just seems more sensible," she said. "Why move everything all the way across town just to get rid of it? This way, you'll carry it from the attic to the curb, and no farther. The garbage collectors will remove anything that's left after your sale. Now I'm going to rest for a while." Mrs. Ross retreated into her bedroom before the girls could thank her again.

Amy and Jan raced up the stairs on tiptoe and silently danced around. "This is terrific!" Amy whispered. "I've already thought up the ad for the paper: 'Giant yard sale this Saturday, ten to three P.M., 35 Post Street. One hundred years' worth of clothes, furniture, dishes, old books, magazines, antiques, treasures. Great deals. Everything must go!' "

The girls were still excited after the long bike ride back to Sugar Tree Acres. As they turned off Roanoke Avenue into the subdivision Amy said, "Hey—hold up! Let's take a look at the clubhouse before we go home!"

"Uncle Robert asked us not to. He wants to surprise us," Jan reminded her.

"He hasn't had time to fix everything. We'll still be surprised," Amy said. "Just a quick look!"

Jan gave in with very little coaxing. "Oh . . . okay!"

They pulled their bikes through a hole in the fence and hurried past the pines and the marsh.

A flock of blue jays scattered, squawking angrily, as the girls stepped into the clearing.

"The plywood's already up on the roof," Amy said. "Let's see how it looks from inside."

But before she could push open the door, the jays started complaining again.

"Maybe somebody's coming!" whispered Jan. "We'd better get back to our bikes. I don't want to disappoint Uncle Robert."

The girls crept out of the clearing and into the trees. Then they heard a high-pitched voice nearby. "It has to be back here. We've looked everywhere else in Sugar Tree Acres!"

"It would be just like the Stars to have their clubhouse in a jungle!" a second voice replied.

"Holly Hudnut!" Jan mouthed to Amy.

"And Brenda!" Amy muttered.

They crouched down behind a maple stump at the end of the marsh and waited. Not half a minute later, Holly and Brenda and Mary Rose crashed through the underbrush.

"Which way?" Holly flipped back her ponytail and frowned.

"There are fewer bushes straight ahead," Mary Rose pointed out.

Holly squared her shoulders. "Follow me!" she ordered.

Jan gasped. "They're going to walk right into the marsh!" she whispered into Amy's ear.

"Shhh!" Amy whispered back. "Come on, Holly," she murmured. "And you, too, Bren. Make my day!"

Holly took one step. The marsh held her up.

"Maybe she's too *petite* to sink," Jan whispered.

But she wasn't. Holly took two more steps . . . another . . . and another . . . and sank in slime up to her ankles!

Brenda was heavier. The marsh got her on the second step.

"Oh, gross! My new pink Antelopes!" Holly wailed as the mud closed over her sneakers.

"This place is booby-trapped!" Brenda howled at the top of her lungs.

"Help us out!" Holly screeched at Mary Rose, who was high and dry on firm ground . . . until she reached for the two unhappy Clovers.

Holly was light, but Holly and Brenda

together were too much for Mary Rose. In seconds the marsh had grabbed her feet too.

Amy and Jan were giggling so much they could hardly stand up.

"Y-you!" Holly yelped when she saw them.

"C-come to visit our c-clubhouse?" Jan stammered with laughter.

"Sorry—no slime allowed," Amy shouted over the Clovers' shrieks.

As the three Clovers clambered out of the marsh, covered with mud to their knees, Amy and Jan ran through the woods to their bikes, giggling helplessly.

◄ 8 ►
Sale Day

Somehow they'd gotten everything done. It was Saturday morning, and Amy and Karen were helping Jan stack platters of brownies—sixteen dozen brownies, to be exact—in the cab of her father's truck. Four dozen brownies had been baked—with Jan's secret recipe—at each of the four Star houses. Amy's mom had even bought sugar for the occasion.

"But if we all used the same recipe, why are some of these so flat?" Amy asked Jan, setting one plate down gently on top of another.

Jan raised her eyebrows and shrugged. "Beth and Sara," she said. "There are so many interruptions at the Greenfields' that anything could have been left out. We'll mix up the batches and hope no one notices."

The Stars had painted signs that said SUPER FUDGE BROWNIES, 75¢ EACH, and they'd borrowed folding tables from Ms. Danner and Karen's parents. They planned to dress up the tables by stapling red crepe paper around the bottoms.

"Thanks, guys," Jan said after they'd lifted the tables into the back of the truck. "See you at twelve thirty." Jan and Sara were starting out at the book fair and Amy, Beth, and Karen were at the yard sale. Then at one o'clock Amy and Beth would go to the library, and Sara and Jan would head to Mrs. Ross's house. "Good luck."

"You too," Amy and Karen said.

They biked back to Amy's house, where Matthew Ellis was sitting on the front steps. Matthew and Pete McBride had insisted on helping the girls carry everything down from the attic, and set it up on the lawn— not because they were such nice guys, but because they wanted to get first shot at it.

"Jan told me there was a moose head in good condition," Matthew said as he, Karen, and Amy climbed into Ms. Danner's van. "How much is it?"

"Matthew, what do you want with a moose head?" Karen asked him.

"You never know when you might need one," said Matthew.

"All ready?" Amy's mother handed her a box full of change. "Let's pick up Beth."

They got to Mrs. Ross's house a little before nine o'clock. Pete was already there, whizzing up and down the sidewalk on his skateboard. He wasn't the only one waiting, either. There were cars with people inside them parked on both sides of Post Street.

"Yard-sale freaks," Matthew informed Amy and Karen. "If you say the sale starts at ten o'clock, they'll be here at eight."

"Good morning!" Mrs. Ross called from her doorway. "Isn't this exciting?"

Amy introduced her mother, Pete, and Matthew. Ms. Danner sat in the living room with Mrs. Ross while the girls and their helpers started lugging stuff downstairs.

"Awesome!" Matthew exclaimed. "I've never seen so much junk!"

"What goes and what stays?" Pete asked Amy.

"Everything goes," she answered, picking up a rickety chair in one hand and a small, cloudy mirror in the other.

"Everything?"

"Everything that isn't in garbage bags," Beth replied, handing him an armload of clothes.

On the front lawn, they piled clothes on top of furniture, spread dishes out on blankets, heaped books onto boxes and magazines into shopping bags. People had started getting out of their cars and edging closer.

"The sale doesn't start until ten o'clock," Amy's mother announced firmly.

"That strange look in their eyes—" Karen murmured.

"It's like sharks, only instead of feeding frenzy it's shopping frenzy," Matthew explained. "Pretty soon they'll begin to circle."

Amy raced upstairs with Beth and Pete to bring down more stuff, leaving Karen and Matthew and Ms. Danner to hold off the crowd.

At ten o'clock on the dot, the stampede

began: dozens of people, pushing, pulling, and grabbing things, came at them.

"Doris, just look at this cup and saucer! Don't you love the color? A dollar seventy-five—I'll take it. And this one too!"

"I have to have that blouse."

"Excuse me, but *I* saw it first!"

"I don't think you did. . . ."

"Here's another one just like it!" Beth jerked a blouse out of a pile near her elbow and handed it to the first woman.

Karen sat on a trunk and made change while Amy, Beth, Pete, and Matthew sold, and Ms. Danner kept an eye on everybody.

Mrs. Ross herself had walked down to take a closer look at the sale when Pete nudged Amy. "Guess who's here," he said, pointing at a shiny blue car pulling up to the curb across the street. SUPRMOM, proclaimed the license plate.

"Mrs. Hudnut!" Amy hissed to Beth.

Holly's mother made a beeline for Mrs. Ross. "Mrs. Ross? I'm Margaret Hudnut. Perhaps you've heard of me. I'm on the . . ." Mrs. Ross nodded uncertainly while Mrs. Hudnut listed a whole string of committees. "But as a trustee of the Committee to

· 87 ·

Preserve Old River Grove," Mrs. Hudnut went on, "I've always wanted to tell you how lovely I think your house is, and . . ."

"Margaret thinks Mrs. Ross is just ducky," Matthew said under his breath.

"One of River Grove's oldest families," said Amy.

"She probably dropped Holly off at the book fair," Beth said.

Karen was peering at Mrs. Hudnut's Mercedes. "No, she didn't—Holly's in the car."

"Wha-at?"

"Holly's in the car—see the top of her head?" said Karen. "I think she's filing her nails."

Mrs. Hudnut picked up the first item her hand fell on, which happened to be a chipped bowl. Talking on and on to Mrs. Ross, she handed Amy's mom a five-dollar bill.

At just that moment Holly glanced across the street. Her mouth made a big round O when she recognized the group.

"Let's give her a large wave," said Pete, grinning mischievously.

"I'm so glad you could come, and so are

the girls," Mrs. Ross was saying graciously while Mrs. Hudnut waited for her change.

The girls? Mrs. Hudnut looked around and for the first time took in Beth, Amy, and Karen.

"They are trying to raise enough money to repair their clubhouse—the Stars, you know."

• • •

"It was great!" Amy giggled.

"Holly looked ready to croak when she saw her mom actually giving the Stars money!" Beth snickered.

"And Mrs. Hudnut flipped out when she realized Mrs. Ross actually knew us!"

Amy and Beth had run over to the book fair to replace Jan and Sara at one o'clock. Booths and tables were spread all over the big vacant lot behind the library. People were selling sandwiches and cakes and lemonade; there was a ring toss, a dunking booth, and a clown makeup stand.

"How are we doing over here?" Amy asked.

"We're almost sold out," Jan replied. "We did have to lower the price on some of the brownies," she added in a low voice, and Amy knew she meant the flat ones. "We've made around a hundred and twenty dollars!"

"When Karen counted the money at twelve o'clock, we'd already taken in three hundred and two dollars at the yard sale!" Amy said. "More than enough to pay back Uncle Robert, and buy some furniture for the clubhouse, and have money left over to give to the library if we want to."

"Three hundred and two dollars!" Jan was stunned.

"Don't you think we should split it with Mrs. Ross?" Sara asked. "After all, it *is* her stuff."

"We tried to talk to her about it, but she wouldn't listen," Amy said. "But we're sure not going to charge her anything for clearing out her attic."

"Matthew was right about yard sales. Remember the Allgood trap?" said Beth. "Pete brought it downstairs because we'd said to bring down everything, and he sold it, with two mice inside, to a little boy. I had to buy the trap back!"

The girls burst out laughing.

"Where are the Clovers?" Amy asked.

"Down at the end." Sara pointed toward the edge of the vacant lot.

There was a big crowd, but Amy could see the top parts of a brown horse, with a little kid on its back.

"Want to take a closer look?" Beth said.

"Not me," said Amy. "I'd much rather remember the Clovers in the swamp than parading around with Missy!"

"The Clovers are charging two dollars for a two-minute ride, and they're making out like gangbusters," Jan reported. "They can probably pay for the whole new wing at the library themselves. It's depressing."

"The yard sale will definitely cheer you up," Amy predicted.

Amy and Beth were selling their last two brownies when someone cleared his throat loudly.

"Uncle Robert!" Amy exclaimed. "What are you doing here?"

"Isn't Jan around?" he wanted to know.

"She's at Mrs. Ross's house. Is anything wrong?" Amy asked him. Uncle Robert seemed awfully quiet. "Did something happen at the clubhouse?"

"The house is okay. Are you girls done?"

Beth and Amy nodded. "No more brownies."

"Let's put the tables in my truck. I'd like to talk to all of you together."

There were just a few stragglers picking through the leftovers at the yard sale on Post Street. Amy spotted the moose head and the yellow shirt with ducks on it under a tree—Matthew Ellis had made his selections.

"Uncle Robert!" Jan cried when she saw him. "Have you finished fixing the clubhouse?"

"It's all fixed, but I have some bad news for you," said Uncle Robert. The tips of his curly mustache drooped sadly.

The girls quickly gathered around. Mrs. Ross and Ms. Danner listened too.

"There are orange flags all over the hill," Uncle Robert began.

"Orange flags?" said Jan.

"Surveyors' flags. When you see surveyors' flags, the bulldozers are usually not far behind." Uncle Robert shook his head. "Somebody must be getting ready to build."

"Excuse me," said Mrs. Ross. "I think I hear my telephone ringing." And she hurried away looking worried.

◀ 9 ▶
The Committee to Preserve Old River Grove

"It's just not fair!" Amy exclaimed. "We have the best-looking clubhouse in the town—make that the *state*—and Piker and Wicket are knocking it down!"

It was Sunday afternoon, and the Stars were admiring Uncle Robert's work at the clubhouse. He'd planed the top and bottom of the front door so that it moved easily, replaced all the broken panes in the windows, painted the frames white, and fixed the hole in the roof so expertly that from the inside, you couldn't tell there'd ever been one. Even from the outside, all you could see was a slight difference in color between the new patch and the old roof.

Uncle Robert had even swept out the leaves and spider webs. The 1879 map of River Grove was hanging over the fireplace.

"It looks beautiful," Sara said sadly.

"Perfect!" Karen murmured.

But just outside a window was a line of wooden stakes with bright-orange ribbons tied to them, marking property lines.

"I think Mrs. Ross was even more upset than we were to hear about it," Jan added with a sigh.

"The longer we hang around, the better we're going to remember this place," Amy said, taking down the map. "And I don't want to. Let's get out of here."

• • •

The girls went back to Amy's house. As they flopped down in the living room, they heard Ms. Danner on the phone in the kitchen. "That's right—at least 1890, maybe older. Right . . . Piker and Wicket. Yes, as soon as possible. . . . Thank you, Bill."

She walked into the living room with a smile on her face. "I don't want to build up false hopes," she said, "but we can get them to postpone the demolition. That'll give us time to work toward something more permanent."

"How, Mom?" Amy asked. "Piker and Wicket own the hill. Can't they tear it all down if they want to?"

"They may own the hill, but the clubhouse is an old building. There are laws in River Grove that prevent people from destroying any structure of historical value," Ms. Danner explained. "I was just talking to my boss, Bill Keeler. We're applying for a restraining order against the developers, which means they can't do anything at all for a certain period of time."

"And then what, Ms. Danner?" Beth asked.

"We'll approach the Committee to Preserve Old River Grove. The committee decides which old buildings are worth saving and which aren't."

There was a chorus of groans from the girls. "But Mrs. Hudnut is a trustee of the committee. We heard her say so just yesterday," Amy told her mother. "A Hudnut would never go out of her way to help out the Stars."

"Margaret Hudnut's an adult. I'm sure she'll behave like one," Ms. Danner replied firmly. "And there are other trustees on the committee besides her. I think they'll be interested in hearing some of the experts who'll be talking at the meeting on Thursday evening."

• • •

Matthew Ellis was wearing the yellow shirt with red and blue ducks on it when Amy walked out to the bus stop on Monday. He was singing along with his Walkman. He'd obviously made another tape from his collection of old 45s, because the words were weird: "Woolly bully . . . woolly bully . . . woo-oolly bully!"

Amy didn't care what Matthew sang, as long as she didn't have to talk to him! If it hadn't been for Matthew, they would never have known about the clubhouse at all!

• • •

The bus ride was quiet. On Monday mornings everybody was half asleep, anyway. But the Stars woke up fast when they stepped through the front doors of the elementary school and heard the noise coming from Mr. Carson's room.

"That's Holly!" Beth said. "What's she yelling about?"

"Take it down this instant!" Holly was standing near the blackboard, screeching at the top of her lungs. A bunch of kids were already in the classroom, some trying to calm Holly down (Brenda and Mary Rose), some laughing like crazy (Cliff Hargrove and the other boys).

"Oh, no!" Karen murmured. The Stars started to giggle.

Matthew had thought of what to do with Mrs. Ross's moose head. It was hung high on the wall, so high that Mr. Carson could hardly reach it, even when he stood on a chair. The head gazed down at the class with its shiny blue eyes . . . and it was wearing a yellow wig with a side ponytail, the Clovers' trademark!

"It does look a little like Holly," Amy muttered, trying to keep a straight face.

"They did it!" Holly shrieked, pointing a finger at Matthew. "Matthew Ellis and Pete McBride. Wait till Mrs. Campesi hears about this!"

"Just a minute, Holly," Mr. Carson said. "Pete isn't even here . . ."

"And Matthew just got off the bus with us," Beth added.

Holly burst into angry tears.

Matthew hummed cheerfully to himself, and Pete slid into his seat one second before the final bell rang.

It would be a while before Holly mentioned mooses again, Bullwinkle or any other kind. And it was the high spot of the week as far as Amy was concerned.

• • •

On Thursday evening Mrs. Greenfield drove the Stars to the town hall, where the Committee to Preserve Old River Grove held its meetings. Amy's mom had left earlier "to pick up a witness," she said.

As the girls filed into the conference room, the first people they saw were Holly and Brenda and Mary Rose, with ringside seats in the front row.

The Stars sat down in the back.

"Since when do the Clovers come to these meetings?" Beth exclaimed.

"Since now," said Amy. "I bet they're just here to see us get dumped on!"

The trustees were grouped around a table at the front of the room. Mrs. Hudnut handed out pencils and pads to the members for note-taking. Then she announced, "The Thursday evening meeting of the Committee to Preserve Old River Grove is now in session. Is there any old business?"

A store owner spoke about the changes he'd made to the front of his building off Main Street.

"We're new business," Amy murmured.

"Where's your mom?" Sara asked nervously.

"Hey!" whispered Jan. "There's Uncle Robert."

He wasn't in his usual work clothes—he was all dressed up in a tweed jacket and pleated pants. He looked gorgeous.

"Wow! Who's that?" the girls heard Mary Rose exclaim as he sat down near the conference table. When Uncle Robert grinned and waved at the Stars, the Clovers turned around and stared. The Stars just smiled.

After the trustees had finished with the old business, Uncle Robert stood up. "My name is Robert Downing," he said. "I have some new business to put before you: a beautiful little house, built almost a hundred years ago at my best estimate, is in danger of being torn down by developers."

The trustees asked him where the house was, what it was made of, and what condition it was in.

"What do you mean by a 'little house,' Mr. Downing?" Mrs. Hudnut asked.

"It might have been built originally as a playhouse for a child," Uncle Robert replied. "In fact, these girls were planning to use it as a clubhouse when I first saw it."

Mrs. Hudnut sighed. "A playhouse! What historical value could a playhouse possibly have?"

"I'll tell you, if I may," came a voice from the doorway.

"Mom brought Mrs. Ross!" Amy gasped.

Mrs. Ross walked slowly toward the table. "I'm getting on, and I don't go out much anymore," she said. "You'll have to excuse me."

No less than five trustees jumped up and offered her a chair.

"You may have heard of me," Mrs. Ross said after she was seated. "My name is Evelyn Ross, but I was a Topping before my marriage. The Toppings were one of the first families of River Grove."

All the trustees beamed at Mrs. Ross and nodded.

"But the Ellison family was here even before we were, and it's the Ellison playhouse Mr. Downing is speaking of. I played in it myself as a girl." Mrs. Ross leaned forward. "The main house on the Ellison estate burned down years ago. The playhouse is all that remains of a family instrumental in founding this city. As it happens, I have inherited a part of the Ellison estate through my husband's relations—the part including the playhouse."

"Our clubhouse belongs to Mrs. Ross?" Sara exclaimed. "Not Piker and Wicket?"

"It's *not* part of Sugar Tree Acres!" Amy said.

"I was approached several months ago by real estate developers who wanted to buy

· 103 ·

my portion of the estate and extend the Sugar Tree Acres subdivison. I had ordered a survey of my property, with the intention of selling to them . . . until I met these girls." She turned to nod at the Stars. "They put me in mind of some of my happiest times as a child—those hours I spent in the Ellison playhouse. So I've decided *not* to sell." She looked sternly at the members of the committee. "If you will see your way clear to granting the playhouse landmark status, I will deed it, and the property around it, to the town of River Grove as a green space."

Amy's heart sank. The clubhouse would be saved, but it wouldn't be *theirs*.

Mrs. Ross went on. "But only after the Stars have used it for as long as they like as their clubhouse."

"What does all that mean?" Beth muttered.

"It's ours!" Karen whispered loudly.

"Mrs. Ross to the rescue!" Amy added happily.

Uncle Robert rushed over to give the girls a big hug, Mrs. Ross beamed at them from her chair in front, and Amy's mom smiled proudly. The Clovers marched past them and out the door without a word.

· · ·

"Pass the mustard," Karen said.

"Did you bring the chips?" Beth asked her sister.

"They're in my backpack, along with the rest of the buns," Sara answered.

The Stars and Uncle Robert, celebrating at the clubhouse with a Saturday afternoon picnic, were roasting hot dogs in the fireplace.

"I wish Mrs. Ross could have come," Jan said. "She would have enjoyed this."

"Once they decide the clubhouse is definitely a landmark, she can come whenever she likes," Uncle Robert said, taking a bite of sour pickle. "They'll put in a road right to the door."

"Yeah." Amy looked around the cozy room at the gleaming new windows, the freshly painted door, the crackling fire in the fireplace and sighed happily. "You gotta admit—when the *Stars* do something, they do it right!"